Sierra the Search Dog Saves Sally

by Robert D. Calkins
Illustrated by Taillefer Long

SIERRA THE SEARCH DOG SAVES SALLY
by Robert D. Calkins

Copyright © 2018 by Robert D. Calkins. All rights reserved.

No part of this book may be reproduced, stored in retrieval systems, or transmitted in any form, by any means, including mechanical, electronic, photocopying, recording or otherwise, without prior written permission of the author.

CALLOUT PRESS
Olalla, Washington
SierraSearchDog.com
RobertDCalkins.com

Illustrations and Design by Taillefer Long
info@IlluminatedStories.com

ISBN: 978-0-9971911-6-5
Library of Congress Control Number: 2018904068

Dedicated to K9 Ruger, who is ably following in Sierra's footprints as a search and rescue dog... very muddy footprints, but footprints nonetheless.

Sierra the Search Dog Saves Sally

by Robert D. Calkins
Illustrated by Taillefer Long

Sally and Sarah were sweet sisters.

They played in the park. They sang in the sun. When it snowed, they went sledding.

Sally and Sarah were totally together in everything they did....except one thing. Sally liked to save shells she collected at the sea shore.

Sarah preferred to sew. She sewed sweaters and socks for family and friends.

One day Sarah was sewing and didn't see Sally leave the house. Sally was going to the shore to collect more sea shells.

But Sally made a major mistake. She didn't tell anyone where she was going.

Sally followed the footpath that wound through the woods. Very soon she saw the shore.

Once on the beach, the sand was so soft, she slipped off her shoes. She wandered and walked but went waaay too far.

Sally found lots of shells. She saved them in a sack. But now the sun was setting. Sally needed to hurry home.

Sally said "bye" to the beach, and walked to the woods. But she took the wrong trail, and that led to trouble.

FUN FACTS

In search and rescue, the human is far harder to train than the dog! As animals, dogs are born knowing how to use their nose to find things. They catch on quickly. Human dog handlers have to learn first aid, two-way radios, how to use a map and compass, and a host of other skills to help the person they find.

The trail was twisty and littered with logs. As Sally stepped over one of the largest logs, she caught her toe and took a tumble. She fell flat, and hurt her hip.

Sally couldn't walk.   She sat and was sad. Her hip hurt and she knew her family would be frightened. She was in terrible trouble.

FUN FACTS

The weather is a big part of search and rescue. Hot air rises, so on hot days, handlers will put search dogs up high, on hills and ridges. On chilly nights, handlers will put their dogs in valleys, because cold air sinks. The goal is to put the dog where someone's scent might be blowing.

As darkness descended, Sarah saw that Sally wasn't home. She found their father and they both wondered and worried whether Sally was safe.

Their father knew they needed to do something. "I know. We'll call Sierra the Search Dog. She'll sniff out where Sally has gone."

FUN FACTS

Dog handlers have to learn to speak in high, squeaky voices called "falsetto" when they're praising their dogs for finding someone. To a dog, a low voice is like growling- a correction. When dogs are happy they yip and squeal, so handlers must learn to play with the dog using a squeaky voice.

Sierra and Bryce were there in mere minutes. They just needed something of Sally's for Sierra to sniff. Sarah ran upstairs. She came back with the comforter she'd sewn for Sally.

Sierra sniffed the soft comforter. Her nose nuzzled it neatly

Once she had Sally's smell, Sierra was off like a shot. She tracked to the trail that led to the beach. She sniffed the sand and found Sally's footprints.

Sierra bounded up the beach. Her nose knew where Sally had gone.

Where the sand was soft, even Bryce could see Sally's footprints with his eyes. He knew Sierra was tracking terrifically.

But where the sand was hard, only Sierra's nose could tell them were Sally had stepped. Bryce said to himself "I must trust Sierra in the sand."

Suddenly, Sierra stopped and started to sniff in circles. Had Sally's scent skedaddled? Had it blown from the beach in a whirl of wind?

FUN FACTS

The scent of a missing person blows through the woods like smoke from a campfire. It's invisible but the dogs can smell it, and follow it back to the missing person.

No! Sierra's nose was working wonders. Sally had spun around with her sack of sea shells. She was obviously heading home. Sierra turned too, and followed her footsteps back down the beach.

But Sally's footprints fell far short of the trail they'd turned from. The trail she'd turned on was nowhere near home, and was noticeably gnarly.

Just as Sally had seen, the trail was terrible. Sierra struggled and Bryce bumped his knee. The leash got tangled around a couple of trees.

Finally Bryce and Sierra found a big tree blocking the trail. Sierra clawed her way onto it, and suddenly could see Sally sitting on the other side.

FUN FACTS

Every single person has their own unique scent. Tiny parts of your skin are constantly falling off, and that's what the dog smells. There can be a trail of those cells on the ground for a "Trailing Dog" to follow. "Air Scent Dogs" sniff to catch your smell blowing on the breeze, and follow that back to the missing person.

"Oh friends, you found me! Who is this pretty puppy in the gorgeous red vest?

"This is Sierra," Bryce said. "She's a search dog. She followed your footprints right to this place."

"Thank you, Sierra!" Sally said with a smile. "It's scary here in the woods. I was afraid I was going to be bitten by badgers or bears. Ohh, I'd have been a marvelous meal."

FUN FACTS

Unless they're actually on a search, you can usually pet a search and rescue dog. Always ask the handler first, but unlike other kinds of service dogs, it's OK to pet most SAR dogs. The more love that search dogs get from people, the more they'll want to find them in the woods!

"Well we're going to help you home," Bryce said to Sally. He broke a branch and made a wonderful walking stick. Sally took a few un-steady steps.

"I think this will work," Sally said. "If the trail is tricky it might be tough. But I'll do my best to not fall on my face."

FUN FACTS

Almost any breed of dog can be a SAR dog, even rescues and mixed breeds. The dog just needs to be big enough to push through underbrush, and have enough stamina to work all day in the woods.

Sally hobbled along even though her hip hurt horribly. Eventually they came to a clearing, and could see Sara on the porch of their house. Sarah ran to see Sally. "Where have you been?

Sally explained she'd taken the wrong trail home, and fallen over a big tree. "Sierra saved me!" Sally said. "She's a search dog!"

"Thank you, Sierra, for saving my sister," Sarah said. She and Sally knelt down, and Sierra gave them both lots of puppy kisses.

They all went back to the girls' house, where they bounced Sierra's ball for her. She gave them even more puppy kisses.

FUN FACTS

If you ever get lost in the woods, sit down and "hug a tree." If you're wandering around, search and rescue dogs might never catch up with you. Stay in one place, and let rescuers come to you.

A few days later, a package appeared at Bryce's house. It had been sent to Sierra. That was decidedly different, because doggies don't get much mail.

Bryce opened the package and out came a comforter- and a thank you note.

The note said: "Sierra- Thank you for saving my sister. I hope this cozy comforter I sewed will keep you wonderfully warm on cold winter nights." It was signed by Sarah.

Bryce put the comforter on Sierra's bed that very night. It was so soft and silky that in no time at all, Sierra was sound asleep.

Soon she started to wiggle and shake. Little barks broke from her lips, and her tail was starting to twitch.

"Doggie Dreams!" Bryce whispered as he too drifted off to sleep. "I wish I knew what you were dreaming about."

About the Author

Robert D. Calkins has been a search dog handler in western Washington state for more than 15 years. Bob currently searches with K9 Ruger, a Golden Retriever who is a nationally-certified search dog. Bob and his dogs have responded to everything from routine missing person cases, to homicides, to the horrific 2014 landslide that swept over the community of Oso, Washington.

Bob is the author of the Sierra the Search Dog series of books for all ages.

About the Real Sierra

Sierra was Bob's first search dog, a Golden Retriever with the well-known "Golden smile" and a natural ability to find people who'd gotten lost. She liked nothing better than running through the woods hoping to pick up the scent of a missing person. Her paycheck was a simple tennis ball, and a scratch on the head. She worked with Bob for five years, responding to many missing person searches in and around western Washington.

About the Illustrator

Taillefer Long is an illustrator and graphic artist based in Charleston, SC. He loves visual storytelling, the creative process, and seeing ideas come to life.

This is Taillefer's fourth collaboration with Robert, with whom he shares a passion for dogs, adventure, and children's books.

Taillefer's work can be found at IlluminatedStories.com

CPSIA information can be obtained
at www.ICGtesting.com
Printed in the USA
BVHW011731010819
R10158100002B/R101581PG554732BVX2B/1/P